THE TRUCKER'S OBSESSION

WORKING CLASS DADDIES

EMMA BRAY

CHAPTER
ONE

Blake

I PULL into the truck stop and put my big rig into park. I sigh and wipe a heavy hand across my brow before I lean my forearms on my steering wheel and look out my windshield.

I can feel the silence of the truck stop, interrupted only by the rumble of my engine as it slowly fades away. The parking lot is empty but for the occasional car and truck, but nothing is moving. It's like no one is here, but I know there are plenty of other truckers here too. They're just probably all asleep in the backs of their rigs.

The sun is setting, casting long shadows across the highway and the parking lot. The dull hum of the buzzing fluorescent lights spills into the air, creating a strange sense of eeriness. The silence is so thick it feels like a blanket, enveloping me in its embrace. I can feel it, like a heavy weight pressing down on me.

There is something hauntingly beautiful about this moment, something that stirs a deep longing inside me. I don't know what it is or why it is so strong, but I can feel it in my bones. The stillness, the solitude, the absolute quiet. I find myself yearning to be part of it, to exist in this moment for just a little while longer.

I reach up and turn off the engine, plunging me into complete silence. The only sound I can hear now is my own breathing, and it's the only thing that I can focus on. I take a few deep breaths, and it feels like I am finally able to relax. I let my head rest on the headrest and close my eyes, taking in the peacefulness of the moment.

The dull hum of the fluorescent lights has become a melody in my ears, and I can feel the entire truck stop like an extension of my own body. I take it all in, from the way the asphalt shimmers in the fading light to the way the shadows seem to stretch out for miles.

I feel the loneliness.

It is a feeling I know all too well, the heavy burden that comes from feeling completely alone. The sun is almost gone now, and the sky is a soft, fading shade of blue.

I exhale another breath and reach for the handle of my truck.

And then I go completely still.

My heart starts beating in overdrive, and every muscle in my body tightens when I see her.

I don't have a clue who she is, but she's the prettiest little thing I've ever seen in all my thirty-two years.

She's an angel.

No, she's a *goddess*.

Her long, red hair flows down over a backpack to an impossibly tiny waist. It's wild and untamed, like a lion's mane. She can't be more than five-foot-four and thin, but she still has a nice handful of curves.

She's nothing short of glorious.

But what the fuck is she wearing?

My cock is a rod of steel as my eyes sweep over her from head to toe. Her white tank top doesn't completely cover her stomach, leaving the expanse of skin just below her belly button and between the hem of her shorts exposed.

And *fuuuck*, those shorts.

They shouldn't even be allowed to be called shorts. They barely cover her ass, and while I'm loving the view, I'm instantly, irrationally enraged and jealous at the thought of other men seeing her like this.

And I know that's insane when I don't even know her.

My insanity goes up a notch when I see several men's heads turn in her direction as she makes her way to the door of the truck stop.

A low growl bubbles up in my throat when I see them blatantly checking her out.

I panic when I see some of them starting to follow her.

Jesus, she's going to start a riot if she's not careful. I see the looks in their eyes. They're thinking the same thing I am, but the difference is I want to take care of her.

I want to be her protector.

And I make my decision here and now.

I fling open the door of the truck and cast threatening glances at every man following her.

She is *my* woman.

CHAPTER
TWO

Alicia

I DON'T KNOW what my plan is. All I know is that I had to get out of *there*.

My stepdad has always been a creep, and now that I'm eighteen, it's all I can do to keep him at bay.

I might be a virgin, but I know what the looks he gives me mean.

And when he started openly palming himself tonight while he looked at me, every alarm in my head started going off —especially when he started drinking.

I didn't know how much longer I could hold him off, so I jetted out of there.

I frown. It's a bit earlier than I wanted to leave. Well, *wanted* isn't the correct term. I've never wanted to be there with him, but, unfortunately, he's the asshole I was left with after my mom split on me.

Yeah, my mom ran off and left me with her new husband. Too bad she never knew who my dad was. I'd rather she had left me with my real father a long time ago instead of the asshat she married and then decided she didn't want to be with anymore.

Apparently, she decided she didn't want to be a mother anymore either.

But I'm not crying about it. It is what it is. She was never much of a mother to me anyway. I always felt like a tag-along, a hindrance to her.

Mom was always more concerned with partying and meeting guys than making sure her daughter was fed and taken care of.

So, I've been taking care of myself for a long time.

And while I never wanted to stay with

Jeff, it was a roof over my head while I tried to scrimp and save what I could to get me a start in life. Plus, it was much better than being in the foster care system. I knew kids who were in it, and as long as I could stay away from Jeff as much as possible, I figured I could put up with his leers.

But he was fixing to start making advances. I could tell.

So, I had to leave sooner than was ideal, but I'm confident I'll be able to make it on my own.

I readjust the backpack on my back. I don't have much in it, just the little bit of cash I made washing cars and the few scraps of clothing I was able to grab before I left my stepdad's.

I don't need much, and besides, too much stuff and I wouldn't be able to carry it all.

My tummy gives a growl. I wish I'd had the foresight to grab a few granola bars at least.

As I step into the truck stop, I'm instantly assaulted by the aroma of food. My mouth starts watering as I glance longingly at the plates of burgers and waffles some of the truckers are eating.

A hot meal looks great, but I chew on my bottom lip as I consider how much cash I have. It would be smarter for me to buy something from the convenience store so I can stretch my money further.

I turn from the diner to head to the convenience store side of the truck stop and gasp when I collide into what feels like a brick wall.

But when big hands reach out to gently grasp my upper arms and steady me, I realize that what I ran into is not a wall but a *man*.

A really, really big man.

My head turns up, up, up to a guy who's got to be at least six-foot-five. He's more than a foot taller than me, and he's nothing but bulging muscle everywhere.

I'm not one of those girls who swoons over super ripped guys, but my face is suddenly flaming, and I feel all sorts of fumbling and stupid.

"Oh," I stammer. "I'm so sorry. I didn't see you there."

He doesn't say anything at first.

Instead, his blue eyes just smolder down at me.

I can't help but stare. I've never seen eyes that color before, and he's got a strong, square jawline, with a firm bottom lip.

But what really blows me away is his hair. It's thick and dark and shaggy, and I wonder what it would feel like to have the strands fall across my bare, aching breasts.

The thought is embarrassingly inappropriate and for a second, I feel myself flush again, but this time there's a different sort of warmth in my belly.

His hands tighten on my arms, and his nostrils flare. I see the muscles in his arms flex, and his chest starts heaving up and down as he continues to stare at me.

"What's your name, dollface?"

I blink, caught off guard but hear myself answer him, "Alicia."

"Alicia." He repeats my name with a note of wonder in his voice, and I press my legs together to ease the throbbing between my legs.

Why am I reacting to this man this way?

My body trembles, and he frowns when he feels it, his eyes skating down over me.

"You cold, honey?"

I melt a little more at the way he calls me 'honey.' And hell no, I'm not cold. I'm on fire, but I nod my head anyway.

"It's no wonder," he grumbles, his eyes heating as they flick over me disapprovingly again. "You're barely wearing anything."

"What?" I stammer as I look down at myself. I'm just wearing shorts and a tank top. "What's wrong with what I'm wearing?"

He barks out a strained chuckle as he leans so close to me his breath skims over my ear, making me shiver again. "Have you not noticed that every man in this truck stop is staring at you?"

My face flames as I turn and look around and finally notice what he's talking about. There *are* several pairs of eyes on me, and they all wear the same lecherous look my stepdad used to give me all the time.

I subconsciously press closer to

whoever this huge man is, my eyes widening when I feel something impossibly hard pressing against my ass.

I tilt my head up to look back at him, and he's staring down at me with a look in his eyes that makes my breath catch.

"You never told me your name," I whisper.

"Blake." His voice comes out husky and rough, like sandpaper.

"Blake," I repeat his name just like he did mine, and I feel that hardness jerk against my backside.

He doesn't even try to hide it. Instead, he growls and grips my hips. "You're enough to start a war, you know that little girl? Who let you out of the house like that?"

I don't know why, but his comments make me flush with pleasure. "No one," I say. "I'm eighteen. I can do what I want."

He pulls me closer to him, subtly grinding that huge part of himself against my ass. "Like hell you can," he growls in my ear where only I can hear. "Look around, honey. These men are hungry wolves, and you're the prey they're wanting to fight over. You need an alpha who's going to protect you."

I peek another glance up at him, my heart racing at his words and his close proximity. This has got to be the craziest thing that's ever happened to me, but I'd be lying if I said I'm not digging every minute of it.

"You're an alpha?" I whisper as he runs his hand down my arm.

He doesn't answer. Instead, he laces his fingers through mine and pulls me along with him towards the truck stop restaurant. I want to question him, but the further we get into the restaurant, the more I'm distracted by how many people are staring at us.

I'm not just talking about the dinner crowd. There's an entire family at the table with their eyes glued to the way Blake leads me to our booth and slams himself in the seat across from me.

Blake ignores them completely, his eyes locked on me. "Stay here," he says.

He leaves me there, stunned and trembling with excitement, and strides to the counter.

I watch as he orders two coffees and two double cheeseburgers with fries.

He carries the food back over to the table and places it all in front of me.

My face flames as my tummy gives another embarrassing growl, but Blake merely orders, "Eat."

I don't try to feign a lack of hunger. Instead, I eagerly obey and dig in like I haven't eaten in a week.

Actually, I haven't eaten much in a week—just cans of soup mostly. I can't really remember the last time I had a burger and fries.

Blake watches every bite I take as he inhales his own food. His eyes never leave me. I feel like I'm the center of attention, and it's not just because everyone is staring at me. It's Blake

He's gorgeous. I can't stop thinking about it. In fact, I don't even want to try to stop.

I don't know how someone can simply look at a person and make them feel so protected and safe. I might be stupid, but I can smell the testosterone and dominance coming off this guy in waves. He's just oozing power, and I want to bask in it.

And then my body reacts. I blush, the color rising all the way up to my roots. I'm almost sure I'm turning the same shade of pink as the hot pink shirt the chick with the red hair and the glasses at the table next to us is wearing.

I bow my head and stare down at my plate as I continue to eat as slowly as I can.

I'm not sure why, but I don't want this to end. I'm not even sure what this is, but I don't want it to end. I want to sit here with Blake and not have to worry about anything other than whether or not I'm going to finish eating this entire burger. I want to sit here with him and muse over the fact that he could probably bench press me.

I'm not sure how long I sit there with my head down, but I know it's too long by the time I look up.

Blake is staring at me with a concerned—almost angry-looking—furrow in his brow. "What are you running from, dollface?"

I consider trying to keep my business to myself and denying that I'm running from anything, but something about this man pulls the truth straight out of me.

"My stepdad."

Blake growls, his hands flexing where he's got his forearms laid on the table.

"Where you planning on going?" he asks me, his voice sounding taut.

"I don't know," I whisper.

His fingers flex again, and his jaw hardens as another growl rumbles up out of that big chest.

Why does that make me clench my legs together?

"Well, I do," he states.

"You do?" I ask, my voice breathless and my eyes wide.

"Yes," his gaze latches onto me as his eyes sweep over me possessively.

"You're coming with me."

Blake

CHRIST ALMIGHTY, this little girl might give me a heart attack. She's so motherfucking innocent. I'd bet my left nut there's never been a cock in her sweet cunt. She doesn't have a clue the stir she's caused coming out dressed in those little shorts, that little teenage virgin pussy of hers practically a siren call to every male within a mile radius.

Christ.

This girl.

She's not even trying to be sexy. She

has no idea that entire ensemble she's wearing is pure *come fuck me*.

She's not wearing makeup. She's not trying to get attention from anyone. What she's wearing is pure *her*.

As I sit down across from her, the only thought in my head is to get her to trust me so I can take her home with me, and then we'll hammer out the details after I claim her.

This little girl reminds me of a kitten. I can take her home, and she'll curl up in my lap, and then I'll pet her until she purrs.

But the longer I sit here, the more I get the feeling that I'm the one who's going to be purring like a contented lion. All this girl has to do is bat those pretty eyes at me, and I'll roll over and let her rub my belly like a pathetic dog.

She's so innocent. She's so sweet. She's so sexy as *fuck*.

She's got me so worked up I'm about to beat my fucking chest.

I'm getting so worked up that my hand is practically shaking.

Fuuuck.

The thought of her stepdad leering at her makes another growl bubble up in my chest. I don't even know the guy, but I want to drag him outside and beat the ever-loving shit out of him for stressing my girl out and making her feel uncomfortable.

And yes, she's *my* girl.

Mine.

I know it deep down in the depths of my soul. I don't know what this is, and I don't really care. All I know is that there's no way in hell I'm ever going to be able to let this girl go.

She's already tattooed deep inside my soul, and there's no getting that out. I'm already so deeply obsessed with her I should probably be worried about my mental state, but I'm not.

A new sense of purpose like I've never known settles over me. I'm going to take care of her and spoil her like the princess she is. I might not be rich, but I make a decent enough living doing what I do, and I'll work my ass off to give her the life she deserves.

I'd do anything for her.

I'll give her the world if I can, and I'll spend every day after that giving her new worlds to explore.

And I'll never give her a reason to look at me with those sad, sad eyes again. I'll never let anyone make her scared or worried again.

That's my promise to her. I'll spend every day of the rest of my life trying to make her happy. I'll try to give her all the good things, and I'll chase all the bad things away.

You hear me, whoever is in charge of this universe?

You better make fucking sure that I get this girl because she is not going to live a life full of misery.

So, if you feel like fucking with her, you better think again, because I'm a fucking machine.

I'll take all those bad things you throw at her and I'll make her smile again.

I'll knock you out like an MMA fighter, and then I'll give her a kiss that cures everything.

I'll give her all the butterflies she's ever wanted in her stomach, and I'll make sure she knows how fucking special she is.

I'll spend my nights kissing away her tears, and I'll be there to give her all the good ones from then on.

I'll be the one who gives her the sunsets, and I'll be the one who gives her the stars.

I'll tell her a thousand times a day how much I love her.

And I'll never, ever give her a reason to doubt me.

She might not know it yet, but she's mine now, and there's no way in hell I'm ever going to let her go.

"I'm going with you?" she whispers, her eyes wide.

And I'm the world's worst bastard because precum spills in my pants at how big her eyes are as she looks at me.

"Yes, dollface. I'm going to take care of you. You'll never have to worry about anything."

She chews on her bottom lip, and I bite back a groan.

"You're killing me, baby," I growl.

Her eyes go even wider. "What?"

I don't elaborate. Instead, I stand and grab her hand, pulling her up to me.

I glance down at the food she's no longer eating. "You get enough, princess?"

She nods, and with that affirmation that my girl's belly is full, I'm ready to get the hell out of here.

There are still many male eyes on my girl. I give each and every one of them a death stare as I pull Alicia close to my side and lead her out of the truck stop's diner and over to my big rig.

I don't put her in the front cab, though. No, there's no way in hell I'll be able to drive with her sweet innocence sitting next to me.

Not until I've at least had the chance to taste her first.

My cock is the size of a coke can in my pants, and it's fizzing over with precum as I open my truck and watch Alicia's ass in those little booty shoots as I help her step up into the back of my truck.

I hop up behind her and close the door before I pull her flush against me, her sweet ass pressed right against my erection.

"You feel what you do to daddy, sweet girl?" I rasp in her ear.

She gasps when I call myself her daddy, but I can't take it back now because something suddenly shifts into place inside me.

That's what I am. This girl desperately needs a daddy. Someone to hold her and protect her and take care of her, and that's exactly what I am.

I'm her daddy. Plain and simple.

"D-daddy?" she whimpers. Her voice is breathy, and I turn her in my arms so that I can see her face. Her eyelids are hooded, and her cheeks are flushed with desire.

Fuuuck. I can't believe what a lucky man I am. My innocent little angel loves me calling myself her daddy.

She's the most beautiful thing I've ever seen, and I can't wait any longer.

I have to taste her. *Now.*

I cup her face in my hands, astounded to find that my hands are shaking. Hell, my entire body is wound up so tight I'm trembling with anticipation.

Her lips part as I lower mine to hers,

and when I feel the sweet give of her flesh under mine, I almost die.

Perfection. She's nothing short of perfect.

My fingers slide down her neck, leaving trails of goosebumps in their wake. I deepen the kiss, exploring her mouth with my tongue. Our breaths mingle, and I can taste her innocence on her lips.

It's intoxicating.

She moans into my mouth, and I know I'm not the only one feeling this intense need.

I pull back to catch my breath, and I see her eyes are dark with desire. I know I shouldn't rush this, but I can't help it. I need her now.

My hands drift down to her waist, and I pull her closer to me. I feel her warmth seeping through the thin fabric of her tank top and shorts, and I know I'm lost.

I break our kiss and pull back to look at her. She's staring back at me with those big doe eyes, and I know she wants this as badly as I do.

"Fuck, baby," I breathe against her

cheek. "How does something like you exist?"

She peeks up at me shyly, her cheeks turning pink, and the sight is enough to send more precum frothing from my tip.

I push her down onto the bed and crawl on top of her.

Our clothes come off in a frenzied rush, and I finally get to see her naked body. She's even more breathtakingly beautiful than I could have ever imagined.

Her little breasts are like perfect cherries. I trail my hand over her flat stomach and to that perfect little mound before sliding them back up to cup her tits.

I lower my mouth to her breasts and take one of her nipples into my mouth. She arches her back and moans, her fingers spearing into my hair, and I know I'm doing something right.

I continue to worship her body, delighting in her every sigh, trailing kisses down her stomach until I reach the spot between her legs.

I part her folds with my fingers and start to stroke her entrance.

"Look at you, baby. You're so wet for Daddy," I praise her.

She bites her lip as she peers up at me, that perfect hair fanning out around her wildly. "Is that good?"

"Yes, baby," I moan. "It's good. It's fucking perfect. The wetter you are, the more I'll like it, babydoll."

Fuck, I can't wait to feel her heat around me.

I kneel down between her legs, practically salivating at the thought of tasting her pussy.

And then I dive in.

I start licking and sucking on her in earnest.

She gasps, her fingers fisting in my hair.

She doesn't scream, but her moans grow steadily louder as I go on.

And I feel on top of the world knowing that I'm making my girl feel good.

I'm focused on making her feel good.

She's so aroused that I can feel her juices dripping down my chin. My cock is so hard it feels like it's going to burst.

Without stopping what I'm doing, I slip one of my hands into my own pants and start rubbing my cock. I'm so excited for this that I don't think I'll last long.

I'll need to come soon.

I go on eating her and rubbing my cock, getting so close to coming that I'm almost there.

It takes all my willpower to stop, but I do because the first time I nut with Alicia, it's going to be inside her pussy, claiming her as mine.

I pull myself up and position myself at her entrance.

"Are you ready for me, babydoll?" I ask her.

She looks into my eyes before she nods trustingly, and that trust nearly guts me.

I don't fucking deserve her. Never in a million years will I deserve her, but I'll damn sure do my best to always give her everything she needs.

I pause for a brief second before plunging in, burying my full length in her.

She cries out as I shred her virginity, her nails digging into my back.

I roar like a warrior, and then my body takes over. I can't stop myself as my hips begin to pump back and forth, plunging deeper and deeper into her sweet depths.

The hard thrusts take my breath away, and I can't help but give in to the primitive urge to own her, to claim her as mine, in the most primal way.

She's *mine*.

I grab her hips and pound into her hard.

She screams, but I feel her throwing her hips back up at me, fucking wanting it as bad as I do.

Fuuuck...

I reach down to touch her clit, and that does it.

"Daddy!" she screams as she comes undone around me, her pussy rippling in waves, milking my cock for all it's worth.

I groan as I follow her over the edge, my release exploding from me.

I collapse beside her, sated, tingling, and so fucking happy.

She's panting beside me. "Daddy," she whispers.

My chest swells as I pull her against

me, feeling her soft body against my bare chest. I kiss her hair and run my fingers over her back. She's so soft and warm in my arms, and I never want to let her go.

I'll *never* let her go.

We lie there, silent for a long time, just enjoying the moment.

I nuzzle her hair and trail kisses down her cheek, petting her until she falls asleep in my arms.

My perfect little girl.

CHAPTER
FOUR

Alicia

I CAN'T BELIEVE this is my life now. Blake swooped in like my prince charming and just took it upon himself to start taking care of me.

He takes me on the road with him and sees to my every need.

I don't know if he has a physical house or not, but it doesn't matter.

We have all we need in the back of his truck. He's got a bed, and he stops frequently to get us food.

Anywhere with him is home to me.

It's only been a couple of weeks, but I already can't imagine life without him.

I love the way he takes care of me. He always buckles me up before he starts driving. He grabs my hand and places it on his thigh while he's driving. Either that or he places his on mine.

It's like he always has to be touching me–and I am more than okay with that.

I love it, in fact.

I love how much bigger he is than me. I love the way he makes me feel cared for and protected.

I know it's fast, but I love him.

We've never said the words, but I think he might feel the same way too.

I wake up to the sensation of my butt sliding across a hard surface, and I open my eyes.

The sun is shining inside his truck, and I can see mountains and trees just outside his window.

My eyes adjust, and I see Blake driving. He's got his shirt off, and his muscular, tattooed arm looks sexy as hell.

I raise my hand to my mouth to cover a yawn as I stretch.

"Hey," I sigh. I watch as his lips tug up into a smile.

"Hey, babydoll," he greets me.

"Good morning," I smile.

"Happy birthday," he adds.

I blink at him in surprise. "How did you know?"

He gives me a heated look. "I know everything about you, Alicia. You didn't think your daddy was going to let your nineteenth birthday come and go without celebrating it, did you?"

I squirm in my seat. "Birthdays were never a big deal to me."

Blake frowns as his hands flex on the steering wheel. "Are you telling me you've never celebrated your birthday?"

I shrug. "Mom was always wrapped up in whatever she was doing, and I've never had a lot of friends, so..." I trail off. It was always hard to make and keep friends with Mom moving us around so much in and out of new boyfriends' houses.

"Well, that's all going to change right now," he says as he pulls into a parking lot. I watch him open the door and hop out of his side of the truck.

He walks around to my side, opens my door, and lifts me out of the cab.

I inhale his scent. God, I love the way he smells. He's got a strong, masculine fragrance that somehow smells of the woods even though we're never in them because he's always driving us.

And I ride along happily with him as he does his runs and makes his deliveries.

He wraps his arms around me as he lifts me and growls in my ear, "I'm taking you to an airplane museum."

My eyes grow wide, and I smile. Blake and I talk all the time when we're on his long drives. I'm touched that he remembered how much I've always been fascinated with airplanes even though I've never been on one.

He plants a hard kiss on my lips and sets me down next to him in the parking lot.

I gasp when I see where we are.

He shrugs his shoulders and grins. "I know it's not a party, but I thought you'd like it."

I bite my lip and nod. "It's better than a party, and it's perfect because it's just the two of us."

His eyes smolder down at me, making me weak in the knees. "Come on, baby-doll," he says as he pulls me into the building with him.

"Wow," I breathe out under my breath as I take in all of the vintage planes in various states of disrepair and repair.

They're all beautiful.

Blake sees me eyeing them and smiles widely.

"Can I climb into one?" I ask.

Blake chuckles. "You can do whatever you want, baby."

I put my hands on the cold metal hull of a fighter jet, and I smile at Blake. "I was just kidding. I'm pretty sure I'm not supposed to climb up in them."

"Well, I wasn't kidding," Blake says as he suddenly hoists me up and deposits me into one of the planes. "It's my girl's birthday, and she's going to do any damn thing she pleases. Anyone who doesn't like it will have to go through me."

I giggle as he gives me a quick kiss and walks around to the plane.

I gasp as I turn and see Blake straddling the tail.

He has his cell phone in his hand, and he's taking pictures of me.

I shrug my shoulders and smile as I run my hands over the pristine plane.

I've never been in a plane before, and this is beyond amazing.

I've always wanted to ride in one, and now I'm sitting in one and can only hope that I'll get to ride in the real thing someday.

Blake snaps another picture of me before he stands up and comes back over to me.

He leans in and takes my lips in a kiss as he grips the back of my neck possessively.

I gasp when I feel his other hand slip down my waist and under my dress to squeeze my bare ass cheek.

"Naughty girl," he growls against my skin. "Does your daddy know you left the house like that, with no panties on?"

I shake my head as I push into his kiss,

loving the way he feels. "No," I whisper huskily. "He'd probably punish me for being a bad girl if he knew."

Blake strokes my pussy, hissing in a breath as he pushes me back so that I'm lying in the plane. His hands come up to cradle my head as he kisses me deeper. "Or, he might reward you for having such a wet little pussy waiting for him."

"Blake," his name comes out shaky and needy—exactly how I feel.

"Happy birthday, babydoll," he says in a rough whisper.

"Thank you," I breathe out. "This is a dream come true."

"Not a dream," he growls. "I'm here. This is real."

I smile up at him as I curl my hand in his.

I want to get out of the plane, but I don't want to have to stop kissing him.

Suddenly, Blake leaps up into the plane and backs me up against the cockpit.

"Blake!" I laugh. "What are you doing?"

His eyes smolder down at me. "I've got you trapped now, babydoll."

My eyes widen at his words, and my heart speeds up in my chest.

Blake always has me trapped.

It might not always be this literal, but he's always got me trapped in his web.

And I love it.

"What do you think you're going to do to me?" I ask.

Blake puts his arm out in front of me and tilts his head like he's going to say something. Then, he shakes his head and crashes his lips down onto me, his hands fisting in my hair.

"Fuck, Alicia, I love this hair of yours. It's beautiful and wild and untamed. Just like you, babydoll. You drive your daddy insane. You know that, honey?"

My heart does somersaults in my chest. The things that Blake says to me...they literally make me weak in the knees.

"I love you," I whisper suddenly, pushing the words out. They tumble from my mouth, but I don't want to take them back. I do. I love him.

"Oh, babydoll," he breathes out against

my lips. "I love you too. So fucking much."

He kisses me again, fiercer than before, as his hand comes down to cup my pussy. He growls lowly in his chest and gives me a possessive squeeze.

"You're so fucking wet right now, Alicia."

I can't control the moan that comes from my throat. I've never been this wet in my entire life. It's Blake. Only Blake can make me feel like this.

His hands are under my dress again, and he growls in the back of his throat when they come into contact with my bare pussy. "I love how slick this little thing is, babydoll, but I need to know that it's mine and only mine."

"It is," I gasp out, thrilling at the possessive, almost manic glint in Blake's eyes. Maybe something is wrong with me, but I love that he's completely obsessed with me. I love that I can make him like this.

He growls down at me, his hand roughly massaging my bare skin. "You're my good little girl, aren't you, Alicia?"

"Yes," I breathe out. "I'm your good girl, Daddy."

I feel Blake's erection jerk through his pants when I call him Daddy, and I can already imagine how much precum it's leaking.

That is one thing I learned about Blake. He leaks a *ton* of precum, and I love it.

All evidence of how much he wants *me*.

"I'm going to fuck you in this plane, babydoll," he growls. "Say you want me to."

"Yes, please Daddy!" I moan.

"I love you," Blake says again. "I really fucking love you, Alicia."

He takes his hand off my pussy and puts it on my head, tangling his fingers in my hair. He pulls my head back, exposing my neck to his hungry mouth. He licks and bites down my neck, and I'm about to come undone. I'm already so close to coming.

I can't think straight. All I can think about is Blake's hands on me. And his mouth. And the slickness between my legs. And that familiar feeling of close, like I'm right on the edge of coming.

"Are you gonna come for me, baby-doll?" Blake's voice is strained, and I can tell it's taking all of his self-control to hold back.

"Yes," I moan. "So close, Daddy! I'm so close!"

Blake's fingers press against my clit, and that's all it takes. I come hard, my hips jerking forward and Blake's hand holding my head still so I'm forced to take his mouth. "Come," Blake growls. "Come all over my fingers, babydoll. Show me how much you love it when I fuck your tight little cunt."

I scream into his mouth, thrashing and shuddering. The orgasm is so intense. Blake's fingers against my clit as I come send me into some kind of nirvana.

When I come back to Earth, Blake kisses me then pulls me into his lap, arranging my body so I'm straddling him. I can feel his erection through his pants, and I whimper at the thought of it. Of him inside me.

I start to wiggle off his lap, but he

holds me still. "Where do you think you're going?"

"To suck your cock," I moan.

"There's plenty of time for that later, babydoll" Blake says, holding me still as I feel his cock jump against my ass at the thought of being in my mouth. "Right now, I want to feel your pussy wrapped around my cock."

I whimper. That sounds good to me too. As much as I love to pleasure Blake by sucking his cock, I love, love, love the feeling of him inside me just as much.

Blake's fingers are still wet from my orgasm, and he uses them to circle my clit before he slips them inside me again. He pumps them in and out of me a few times, making me moan, before he says, "I'm going to fuck you hard, babydoll. You ready for that?"

"Yes, Daddy," I moan. "Please!"

Blake stands up with me in his arms, our lips still pressed together. My arms are around his neck, and his are around my waist as he walks us right over to the window.

"Get on your knees," Blake orders.

I whimper. I've never done anything like this before. I'm very aware that we're in a public place and doing something that we probably shouldn't, but I'm not scared.

Because I know my daddy is in charge and he's always going to take care of me.

I bend down. Blake helps me, his hands at my waist, pressing me against the window. He pulls my dress up to my waist and I lean forward, bracing myself on the window with my palms.

"Fuck," Blake says, his voice filled with awe. "Look how wet you are, babydoll."

I look down and see the glistening evidence of my arousal.

Blake leans over me and strokes his fingers through my slit, spreading my juices all over my pussy and making my clit throb. "Beautiful little thing," he growls, and I moan as he sticks his thumb in my mouth.

"Suck," he commands.

I suck, tasting myself on Blake's skin. His cock throbs against my ass, and I wiggle again, trying to encourage him to give it to me.

He pulls his thumb out of my mouth, and I gasp as I feel the tip of his cock at my entrance. He slides it all the way in, and I gasp at the feeling of him filling me. I'm desperate to feel him moving in and out, and I'm trying to silently beg him for the friction, but all I can do is gasp and whimper.

Blake's voice is strained and husky when he grunts out, "Tell me what you want, baby."

"Please, Daddy," I moan.

"Please what?"

"Please fuck me."

Blake immediately thrusts deeper inside me, hitting that spot that makes me see stars. He groans as he starts to pump me slowly, making me whimper at the pleasure he's giving me.

But then, he picks up the pace, fucking me hard and fast, and I'm moaning and whimpering endlessly, loving every second of it.

My body is on fire, and I try to brace myself on the window as Blake pumps me, but my knees are trembling too much, and I can feel myself losing my balance.

The only thing I can focus on is the feeling of Blake's cock thrusting and stroking me from the inside out. My pussy is throbbing and pulsing, and I know I'm on the edge of a powerful orgasm.

Blake starts fucking me even faster, and I feel my orgasm approaching. It's right there. I'm so close to the edge I can practically taste it, but I don't want to come without Blake.

I can feel his cock throbbing inside me, and I know he's close to coming too.

"Come on babydoll. Come for Daddy," Blake whispers hotly in my ear, and that does it.

I scream, my fingers digging into his arms as my pussy clenches and clamps down on his cock.

Blake's groans are distorted by the window as he slams his length inside me once more, and then I feel him.

He fills my pussy with his cum, and I moan as I feel him emptying his balls inside me.

We're both shaking as we struggle to catch our breath. I feel Blake pull his cock out of me, and I whimper, wanting him back in me.

He takes me into his arms and tucks me to him. He's still hard, and I know he could easily get hard again and fuck me again, but he seems content to hold me for the moment.

"You like being fucked hard and dirty by your daddy on your birthday, baby?"

"Mmmhmm."

Blake places a tender kiss on the top of my forehead. It's the kind of kiss that makes me feel loved, safe, and protected.

"I love making you feel good, Alicia." I hear the sincerity in his voice.

I smile to myself. "I know you do."

"Who's there?"

I hear a voice that makes me stiffen, my body going cold.

No...

It can't be...

I pull away from Blake and gasp as my suspicions are confirmed.

It's my stepdad.

CHAPTER
FIVE

Blake

ALL MY SENSES go on high alert as Alicia goes completely still in my arms. Her face pales, and she begins to shake.

My eyes zero in on the asshole who interrupted us, and I instantly know who he is.

Of course, I did my homework and found out who Alicia's stepdad was.

I don't know what the fucker is doing here, and I don't care. If he so much as breathes in my Alicia's direction, he's a dead man. Hell, he might be anyway.

Alicia went from happy and sated to on edge in seconds, and it is taking all of my self-control to keep my shit together. One look at the expression on her face, and I know that she's scared.

That infuriates me. I hate the source of anything—and most especially any*one*—that makes my girl feel this way.

I pull her closer to me, and when I run my hand up her back to comfort her, my fingers feel the goosebumps.

"Alicia?" Her stepdad blinks in surprise before his eyes flick to me and narrow.

"Where have you been, baby girl? Do you know this man?"

Her stepfather has this calm, collected voice, but I can hear the undertone of anger.

Well, his anger can't match my own at hearing another man call *my* girl, baby girl or any other endearment.

"Yeah, she does," I answer for her as I splay my hand against her back and rub soothingly. "Who the fuck are you?"

I can tell he doesn't like being questioned, but I don't give two fucks. I'm about to kill the fucker, and if I have to die too, then I will happily meet an early death. No one talks to, looks at, or touches my girl.

My hand tightens around Alicia's waist, and she settles in my arms. I don't let go of her. She relaxes slightly, no doubt sensing my righteous anger.

The man straightens in an effort to look authoritative. "I'm her stepfather. I've been worried sick about her."

His gaze flicks over to her, and I step in front of her to block his view, my anger boiling just below the surface now.

"There's no need to worry about her. She's being well taken care of."

I see the man's eyes flare as he takes me in. His gaze slides over me slowly, and he swallows hard.

You'd think the idiot would have enough sense to simply walk away now.

But no.

He pushes the envelope.

Like I knew he fucking would.

"Oh yeah? By who?"

"Me." I widen my stance and square my shoulders.

The man's gaze flicks back and forth between Alicia and me, his face turning redder and redder by the second until he finally bursts out, "You ungrateful little brat. I've played daddy to you ever since your piece of shit mother left, and this is how you repay me? By running off with the first dick you find and letting him keep you like some common whore?"

And that's what makes me lose it. Her stepdad doesn't realize it, but he's given me just the excuse I need to wipe the floor with him.

He's called Alicia a slut, and that's unforgivable.

He'll die. Today. *Now.*

I grab Alicia by the waist and lift her up so I can carry her bridal style.

She doesn't even try to stop me.

Instead, her arms wrap around my neck, and she buries her face in my chest.

I'm glad she can't see me right now.

I don't want her to see me like this.

I'm about to kill a man, and I hate that she might think I'm capable of doing such a thing, even if I know deep down that she knows me better than to think I'd ever hurt her.

The man pulls a gun out and points it at me, and I hear Alicia gasp from behind me.

My response is gratifyingly swift.

I hide Alicia behind the plane. Then, I'm on him faster than you can blink, my fists flying.

I punch him in the gut.

He doubles over in pain.

I punch him in the face.

He goes down like a ton of bricks.

Someone shouts from behind me, but I'm already turning to face the one who dared to raise his voice to me.

Alicia's stepfather is down.

Someone else wants to take his place.

I don't give a fuck who the man is.

If he wants to take a shot, he's got one.

I'm looking forward to it.

I'll do *anything* to protect my Alicia, and right now *everyone* is a threat to what's *mine*.

Suddenly, Alicia's hands are cupping my face, pulling my eyes down to hers.

My breathing calms as I focus on her

innocent eyes. I stare into them, allowing myself to dive deep into their depths, imagining them as waves washing soothingly over me.

"Blake," she calls my name softy. "Please, let's get out of here."

She doesn't have to ask me twice.

I ignore the museum workers still arriving on the scene as I scoop my girl back into my arms and march her toward the door.

I buckle her back up in my big rig and hit the road, my only intent to get us far enough away from her stepdad that I can think clearly again. Pushing the gas pedal to the floor, I quickly hit the limit, then keep going over it so I can put as much distance between us and the museum as I can.

Alicia doesn't speak as I drive. My entire body is still coiled with tension, but she eases it by keeping her little palm pressed against my thigh.

I place my free hand atop hers and hold it there, needing her touch to reassure me she's here. She's safe.

With *me*.

No one is going to hurt her or take her away from me.

I'm not going to let that happen.

When I finally calm down enough, I drive her to my home for the second half of her birthday present.

I hate that her piece of shit stepdad marred the first, but I'm going to do everything in my power now to erase every memory she has of him.

I see Alicia surveying my home curiously as I park the big rig in my driveway.

It's not much, and I'm not here often, but I never sold my dad's house after he died and left it to me, figuring I'd always have a place to call home if I ever wanted a break from the road.

I've never had a reason to take a break.

Until now.

Now that I have Alicia, I have a reason to slow down and live again. I no longer have the need to lose myself on the road. I'm not rich, but I'm not extravagant either, so I've banked most of the money I've earned trucking over the years.

I've got enough saved up to make Alicia's dreams come true. I've got enough saved up to take a long break and spend time with my girl.

The woman I'm going to make my wife.

"Is this your place?" she asks me.

I nod. "Yeah, babydoll. This is my home." I walk around and let her out of the truck, taking her hand as I lead her through the door.

It's nothing fancy, but it's big enough for just me.

And now her.

"Come on," I urge as I pull her into the kitchen. "You hungry?"

She nods, and I smile.

"I'll make you dinner then. How does spaghetti sound?"

She nods with a smile, and I whip up a meal that's worthy of a five-star restaurant. As I cook, I can feel Alicia's eyes on me, and I can feel her nervousness from across the room.

I know she's worried that she's imposing, but she has nothing to worry about. I want her here.

I *need* her here.

When I finish cooking, I set the food on the table.

Alicia gives me a smile that takes my breath away. "How do you remember everything? That I love planes. That spaghetti is my favorite."

"I remember everything about you, baby," I tell her solemnly. If she only knew just how obsessed with her I am...

We eat in a companionable silence, the only sound breaking it Alicia's moans of approval.

My cock lengthens in thickens in my pants as I watch her. Christ, the girl can make something as innocuous as eating sexual.

The way her lips wrap around the fork, the slurping noises she makes when she sucks a noodle into her mouth...

Those fucking moans...

I'm ready to nut in my pants right now.

Better yet, I'm ready to throw her across the table and eat her out like she's the main course.

But first, I want to give her the last

part of my birthday gift to her. Anything to make my girl happy...

"Alicia," I finally say softly. "You know how you always wanted to become a stewardess?"

Her face lights up with excitement at the mention of her old dream, and she nods eagerly.

"I want to pay for your education," I continue, my voice thick with emotion. "I want to give you the chance to make that dream come true."

Alicia's mouth drops open in shock, and tears begin streaming down her soft cheeks. She chokes out a few words of disbelief before she throws her arms around me, burying her face into my chest as she weeps from joy.

For a moment, we just stand there embracing each other in the middle of my kitchen.

"I don't know what to say," she finally murmurs against my neck.

"I told you your daddy would always take care of you," I tell her huskily.

She presses closer to me and then

looks up at me shyly when she feels my erection between us.

"How ever can I repay you, Daddy?"

And just like that, precum starts spewing from my tip. All it takes is this beautiful girl calling me daddy in that innocent little baby girl voice of hers, and I'm ready to blow.

I groan when Alicia takes the initiative, drops to her knees, and begins fumbling with my zipper.

"Good girl," I groan when she finally frees my throbbing length. It bobs free, drooling sticky ropes of precum that Alicia happily begins lapping up like a kitten with a bowl of cream.

I can't help but groan as that tiny mouth of hers engulfs the head of my cock.

"Daddy, this is the best birthday present ever," she coos around my hardening shaft.

"And it's the least I could do for you," I tell her as I fist her hair gently, holding her in place so I can thrust my hips and feed her more of my dick.

"Mmmm," she hums, sending vibrations down my cock.

My cock jumps in response, and I feel my load starting to work its way up my shaft.

"Alicia, baby, your daddy's gonna come," I warn her.

She just whimpers softly and quickly doubles her efforts, bobbing her head up and down my shaft as it pulses in her mouth.

"Fuck, little girl. Play with that pretty little pussy. Come first before your daddy does."

Alicia's hand immediately moves between her legs to obey.

She whimpers around my cock, and I strain with the effort it takes to hold back.

"Come for me, babydoll," I beg her, desperate for her to come first.

She obeys like the perfect good girl she is, and I can't hold off any longer.

"You want to get a big, sticky load of Daddy's cum in your mouth?" I grunt as I grab her head.

"Mmmm-mmmmm!" she moans in understanding, and then she furiously works my cock, sucking on my head and bobbing up and down my shaft.

"Fuck, baby girl," I hiss. "Daddy's gonna come so fucking hard."

"Mmmm-mmm!" she moans in delight.

And then I blow.

I throw my head back and groan like a wounded bear as I blast rope after rope of hot cum into the back of her throat. She gags as I stuff her mouth full of my throbbing cock, but she quickly recovers and begins working it with her tongue, swallowing my hot, sticky cum with the same enthusiasm as if she's trying to earn an A+ on an exam.

"Fuck, babydoll," I groan as I pull her up to me and wrap her up in my arms. I kiss her forehead, my heart full with everything I feel for her

"Daddy's so proud of you for being such a good girl," I coo into her ear, giving her the praise and aftercare I know she basks in. "I love you so much."

"I love you, too, Daddy," she replies, sounding a little hoarse from the enthusiastic cock-sucking she just administered.

"And I'm always going to take care of you. Forever."

She beams up at me happily as she nods and repeats. "Forever."

And I now know that I'm the luckiest daddy in the world.

EPILOGUE

Two Years Later

Alicia

I STAND in front of the mirror, adjusting the cheerful blue skirt and white top of my new uniform. I smile as I think back to when I first met Blake and how my life has changed since then. Just two short years ago, I had fled my stepdad's. I had nothing, and there's no telling what would have happened to me had it not been for Blake.

Thanks to him and his encouragement,

I've achieved my dream job of becoming an international flight attendant for one of the world's best airlines.

My new job is everything I ever dreamed it would be. Every day is an adventure, every destination another story waiting to be told. I love the feeling of anticipation that comes with every takeoff and every landing, the thrill of soaring through cloudless skies and gazing down at stunning landscapes from thousands of feet up. It's exhilarating!

And while it wouldn't have been possible without Blake's support, what really makes this job so special is that he often joins me on trips.

We've been able to visit some amazing places together over these past two years. Paris, Spain, London... Not only do we get to explore some incredible cities together, but we also get to sleep side-by-side in luxurious hotel rooms and make love beneath foreign stars each night.

I smile as I walk to the back of the plane where my husband sits. His eyes are trained on me every step of the way.

I already see the prominent bulge in

his pants, and I feel an answering throb between my legs.

He smirks when he sees me press my legs together.

"You're going to be late for your pre-flight briefing, babydoll," he points out with a teasing grin.

I look down at the floor of the plane meaningfully. "You're not."

He groans as I drop to my knees next to him and unzip his pants.

The plane will be boarding soon, so we can't exactly do this right here.

But I can give him a preview.

He groans as I wrap my lips around his dick.

As I suck him, I glance up at him and run my hands through my hair. He's watching me with such love in his eyes. My heart flutters as a single tear crawls down my cheek and falls onto his throbbing shaft.

He reaches over and wipes it away, resting his hand on the side of my face.

"I love you, Daddy" I whisper, gazing into his eyes.

"I love you, too, baby. You're the best thing that ever happened to me."

I smile as I pull his cock into my mouth once more and give him the best blowjob of his life.

I live to please him.

He's everything I never knew I needed.

My daddy. My lover. My husband. My *everything*.

Want more Emma Bray? Go to www.authoremmabray.com to sign up for Emma's newsletter and get a free book!